It's Church Going Time

By Wade Hudson
Illustrated by Peter Ambush

MARIMBA BOOKS
An imprint of Kensington Publishing Corp. and Hudson Publishing Group LLC
850 Third Avenue, New York, NY 10022

Text copyright © 2008 by Wade Hudson. Illustrations copyright © 2008 by Peter Ambush.

ISBN-13: 978-1-60349-005-4   ISBN-10: 1-60349-005-1
First MARIMBA BOOKS Printing: October 2008

10 9 8 7 6 5 4 3 2 1

Printed in the United States of America

MARIMBA BOOKS

Ma Dear starts singing early on Sunday morning.

He's got the whole world in His hands.
He's got the whole world in His hands.

Her soothing, mellow voice fills the kitchen with happy melodies.

She claps her hands to keep the beat. Even the bacon and eggs cooking on the stove seem caught up in the rhythm.

"It's church going time, Taj," she says.
"Today is Sunday and this is our time to go
and praise the Lord!"

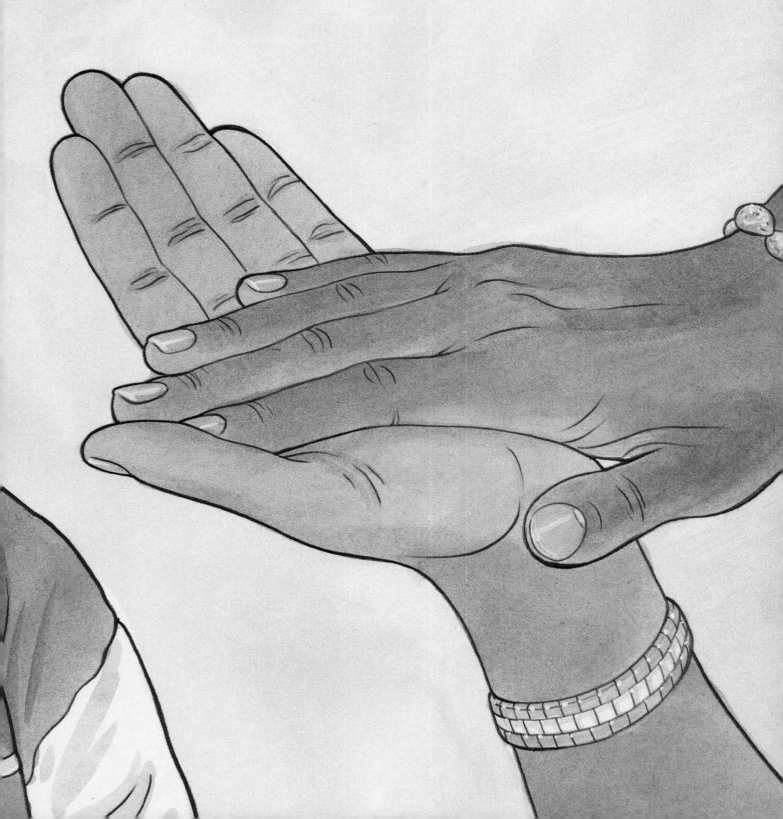

Every Sunday I ask my grandmother the same question.

"Ma Dear, why are you always so happy on Sunday morning?"

She puts a delicious buttered biscuit on my plate. Then she serves me scrambled eggs and bacon.

"Taj, I told you.
Today is church going time."

Then Ma Dear sings another one of
her favorite spirituals.

> *I'm so glad, Jesus lifted me.*
> *I'm so glad, Jesus lifted me.*
> *I'm so glad, Jesus lifted me*
> *Singing, glory hallelujah, Jesus lifted me.*

"But why do we have to go to church?"
I ask as I take a bite of my biscuit.

Ma Dear stops right in the middle of her song. She grabs my hand and squeezes it.

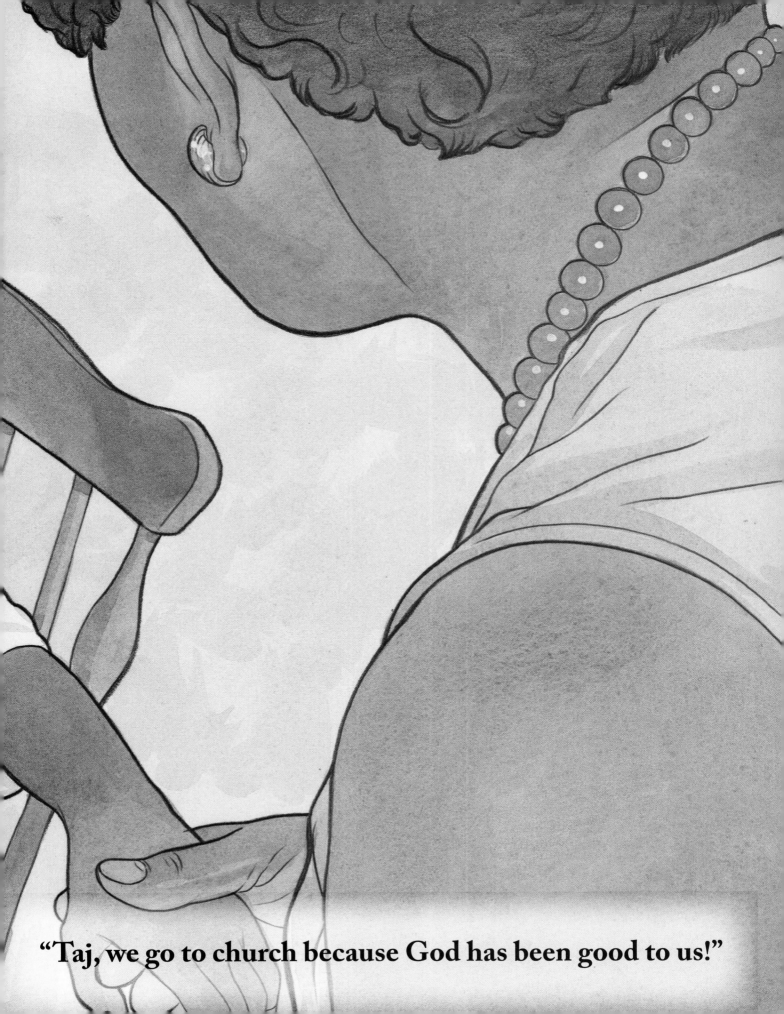

"Taj, we go to church because God has been good to us!"

She looks me straight in the eyes.

"Going to church is one way to show the Lord our thanks."

Then Ma Dear seems to drift away from me.

She settles in her special place. It's like the place I go to in my mind when I remember something very special...like the time I made the shot to win the basketball league championship.

"Taj, I just love to hear the church choir sing.
I need the peace that the altar prayer brings."

"Holy Communion renews my faith.

And the pastor's sermons teach love, not hate."

"The ushers greet me with a welcoming smile.

The deacons stop and chat for a while."

"There are friendly faces everywhere.

That's because God's spirit is there."

Ma Dear places a cold glass of milk next to my plate. But I can see that she is still in her own special place.

"You know," she says, "church is where your father got his first chance to speak in public. I can still remember the speech he gave on Youth Day."

A warm smile brightens her face.

"Taj, I love my church just like I love our home."

Soon, Ma Dear and I are off to
Imani Baptist Church of Christ.

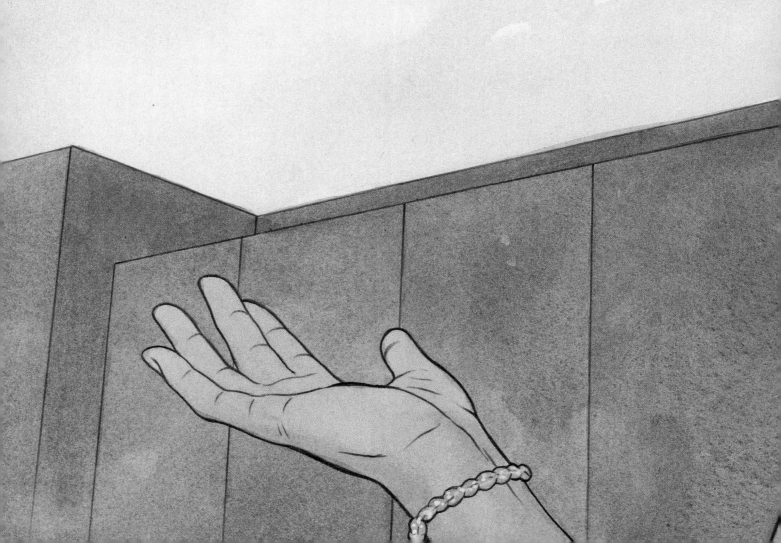

"You look blessed this morning, Mrs. Cummings."
"It's so good to see you."

The greetings are warm and caring.

A warm smile brightens Ma Dear's face again as we enter the sanctuary.

She is home.

I smile, too, because I like hanging out with my grandmother—especially when it's our church going time.